'Humour, wisdom, narrative power... [Čolić] leads us up the garden path. For our own pleasure'

Télérama

'This account of the tragic life of Amedeo Modigliani enables you to enter his Montparnasse studio, smell the colours of his paint and empathically share the poetic space of a beautiful and damned soul from the Tyrrhenian shores'

Bianca Sforni

VELIBOR ČOLIĆ was born in Bosnia in 1964. Since 1992 he has lived in France as a writer and freelance music journalist. *The Uncannily Strange and Brief Life of Amedeo Modigliani* has been translated into French, Italian and German, and adapted as a radio play.

VELIBOR ČOLIĆ

THE UNCANNILY STRANGE
AND BRIEF LIFE OF
AMEDEO
MODIGLIANI

A Mosaic Novel

Translated by
Celia Hawkesworth

PUSHKIN PRESS

Pushkin Press
71–75 Shelton Street
London, WC2H 9JQ

The Uncannily Strange and Brief Life of Amedeo Modigliani was first published as
La Vie fantasmagoriquement brève et étrange d'Amadeo Modigliani in France, 1995

First published by Pushkin Press in 2011
This edition first published by Pushkin Press in 2018

3 5 7 9 8 6 4

ISBN 13: 978 1 78227 497 1

Offset by Tetragon, London
Printed and bound by CPI Group (UK) Ltd, Croydon, CRO 4YY

www.pushkinpress.com

THE UNCANNILY STRANGE
AND BRIEF LIFE OF
AMEDEO
MODIGLIANI

What does it matter if radiance, which was once so vivid, has now been forever banished from my sight. And although nothing can bring back that instant of brilliance in the grass and splendour in a flower, we shall not regret it, but rather we shall draw strength from all that has been left us. We shall draw strength from primeval compassion which, since it has always existed, will continue—in the dying thoughts that well up from human anguish, in the faith that devours death, in the years that bring a philosophical understanding of the world.

For Mary-Jane [1956–90]
with all my love that proved inadequate …

Paris, Rain

A T LAST, on the twelfth of August 1919 AD, it rained. Lolotte came along the west side of the street, bringing a scorched wreath, virtually dry, of cows' eyes for lunch.

The first morning shadows—those clearest ones, the most sharply defined—occasioned by the unexpected gloom outside—played over the wall, and then over the long, tormented face of Amedeo Modigliani, fading on the unfinished canvas where there was a prostitute with a pockmarked face. Eyes without pupils.

Then the painter, coughing, dishevelled reached for a knife with an ornamental handle of soft rosewood and drove it despondently into the angelic and sensuous left arm of the girl who screamed. I watched as though hallucinating, said Leopold Zborowski later, as a piece of flesh, white as mutton, fell onto the wet street, alarming the drunken Cocteau, some prostitutes and a bow-legged Arab angel. Then I bounded up the stuffy stairway at a run to find the drunken Amedeo and the frightened Miss Lolotte in a tortured and indecorous position of animal coitus, while a thin red thread trickled down the girl's left arm, leaving marks like rust on the floor.

Dusk found the three of them drinking wine and discussing Cézanne, Toulouse-Lautrec and the delicacy and elongated form of African statuettes. Then Amedeo Modigliani talked about Lodovico di Vartemi, a nobleman from Bologna, who wanted to reproduce faithfully something he had seen in 1505 on a journey to Calcutta, a celebration of the festival of the twenty-fifth of December consisting of a circle of illuminated fir trees placed around a temple.

Zborowski hiccuped and reminded them that he was a Catholic.

Lolotte laughed and went to pee in another part of the room.

The two men closed their eyes.

Poppies, Dream

MONTPARNASSE, AFTER RAIN, breathing deeply. Two men who are immigrants bring into that same room a considerable quantity of opium from Afghanistan, which makes the thinner and taller of the two, Nekrasov, leaning on the door-post, find it hard to breathe—he coughs yellow mucus into a stained handkerchief.

He asks about the rust on the floor.

The ones who live there say nothing.

The two men who are immigrants leave the opium and vanish with a 'bye into the darkness of the stair-well. In the street the thinner and taller of the two, Nekrasov, steps with a rat's caution round a lusty ultramarine lady, who has eyes without pupils, who is in fact the embodiment of death—the worst kind: immigrant death. Death with no funeral service, no requiem, death with foreign clay in one's mouth. Inside, Zborowski and Lolotte are kissing.

Modigliani, high by now, sees a vision of poppies in his native Livorno. Since they have no champagne left, Zborowski and Lolotte move closer together.

Intimately.

Afterwards Zborowski places Amedeo Modigliani on his low, fairly dirty iron bed.

But Amedeo's head falls off the pillow.

Zborowski puts it back.

Fear, Dream I

WITH A COMB, the woman removes the top of the angel's head. Jeanne Hébuterne tattoos poppies and marigolds on the inner side of her waxy thigh.

It is summer but there is no sun in the sky.

Her eyes have no pupils either.

He dreams that he is stepping between his eccentric fellow countrymen, Italians, who are carrying a Madonna, naked, raped, on an improvised cross.

She bears an incredibly close resemblance to Jeanne.

He tries to explain that they are wrong.

They tell him to fuck off, signore.

Utterly confused and terrified, Amedeo Modigliani turns and runs across a field full of poppies. He looks up and sees the angel with no top to his head painting the sky blue.

He hears his eccentric fellow countrymen, Italians, praising their own masculinity.

He wakes and goes over to the table.

The water is stale.
He drinks it and glances outside, at the sky.
The sky is grey.

Morning, Hunger I

JEANNE HÉBUTERNE is not the same as she was in the dream—
In reality she is far less real.

And then, as though compressed by the morning, the two of them have breakfast, the lascivious red-haired woman with eyes without pupils, Jeanne Hébuterne, and the thin, hung-over painter, the Italian vagabond Amedeo Modigliani. They eat the sparse cockroaches from behind the wallpaper, knights of the kitchen table, with salt, and drink stale water on the surface of which float fat drowned flies, black, almost dark blue with their legs turned towards the sky.

Jeanne lifts up her skirt and shows him the bird.

And then, as though compressed by the morning, they put salt on the young pheasant's tail, scatter ashes over its head and big peppercorns on its impotent wings.

Then, they tear it apart and eat it greedily, while it's still warm.

There are feathers everywhere.

Oh well, fuck it, she says, it's raining at last.

Of course, he says.

Then they roll, light and smoke olive leaves, laurel and a strange Indian plant. The smoke fills the space, cramped but crammed with furniture, which is sparse and consists of
—a fairly low bed
—a rickety little table with a bottle and kitsch candlestick
—a cement floor, stained in places with spit,
windows (two) with three panes
—and an easel and paints.

They listen to the landlady, Madame Carmelita with the triple stomach, giving birth on the floor below, to her seventh child, emitting from her throat sounds resembling a wounded sow.

They smoke again.

Drawing a huge, elephantine, mouthful of smoke into his already damaged lungs, Amedeo Modigliani gets up, goes over to the easel and brings back paints
—sickly yellow, the colour of tuberculosis,
—Parisian blue, the colour of Montparnasse after rain
—and ultramarine, the colour of her eyes and veins.

They swallow them.

His nudes and partially draped female figures are among the most sensuous and beautiful in the whole of art.

H H ARNASON

Carmelita, Children

CARMELITA, THE LANDLADY with the triple stomach, first gives birth to Sebastian, a little boy, then, ten minutes later, tormented by an insidious pain below her navel, climbs up to the floor above hers squealing like a wounded sow, banging with both hands on the locked door through which some kind of smoke is emerging—exactly like incense.

Open up, she says, fuck your drugged mother.

From the other side of the door comes silence.

Open up, she says, and pay your rent.

Fuck off old woman, says the painter without opening the door.

Carmelita, the landlady with the triple stomach, turns away swearing and runs down the dark stairs muttering about hell, muttering about the devil, muttering about someone's thieving mother, muttering about prison.

Muttering about the police.

At that precise moment, barefoot, her sister Donna Clara is leaving their native Puerto Rico.

From somewhere comes the music of the spheres. In the street a lot of people watch the fat woman in astonishment.

Crime, Punishment

YOU'RE A MONKEY, says Jeanne in English.

He doesn't understand her.

You're a monkey, she repeats.

He looks at her.

Jeanne is as beautiful as a soldier's longing, beautiful as candle wax, as life itself, beautiful as the strong, atavistic bonds between man and the earth, deep, cosmic, simply

—beautiful.

Wisdom, she says, lies in tearing out the heart as soon as possible, before sorrow settles in it.

Otherwise it's too late.

Of course, he says.

The police find them, together, the two of them, in the first flare of twilight, completely naked, painting long phallusoid candles on the wall with yellow paint, the sickly colour of tuberculosis.

Enough fucking around, say the policemen.

Amedeo Modigliani drops his paintbrush, turns and looks blankly at the gentlemen with moustaches.

Get ready, they say.

Ten minutes later, he sets off down the dark stairway, treading slowly, at an almost funereal pace, accompanied by the tense gentlemen with moustaches.

I'd read, of course, that in gaol one ends up by losing track of time. But this never meant anything definite to me. I hadn't grasped how days could be at once long and short. Long, no doubt, as periods to live through, but so distended that they ended up by overlapping each other. In fact I never thought of days as such; only the words 'yesterday' or 'tomorrow' still kept some meaning.

ALBERT CAMUS *The Outsider*

Night, Day

A MEDEO MODIGLIANI, with no paints or brushes, spends almost the whole of his first night in prison thinking of revenge. He considers ending Madame Carmelita's piglike life with blows of a knife—one with an ornamental handle of soft rosewood—to her neck, her face, her body, everywhere.

And filling her body with pearls.

The night is as long drawn-out as hunger.

At ten o'clock at night the drunken guard finally brings him supper.

Amedeo Modigliani refuses the food, just takes the water.

The guard talks about the way dreamers often die of hunger, thus proving that they lived on dreams.

The painter says nothing.

Then he sleeps and dreams of a prostitute.

Fear, Dream II

WHILE HE PLACED his lips on her cheekbones. While there in the dark he broke the silver of her neck.

While the pallid strips of skin of his upper lip traced the form of her breast.

While he made round nests in her hair and under her navel.

While he hushed Venus with his palm.

While he connected his lungs to the sky with the tip of his cigarette.

While he counted the moles on her body.

While he roused her breathing, her soft, sheep-like, white breath.

Lolotte was a young boy.

Lolotte was a shepherd.

While he made discoid swallows of her blonde curls.

While he whistled about elephants.

While he transplanted motherhood into her apple.

While he made a circus at her feet.

While he listened to how fluid and juicy she was inside.

While he settled the wind in her flaming nostrils.
While he made her into a flamingo.
While his hips moved up-down-up-down-up-down.
While he smelt of chestnuts and seed.
While he roused her breathing, her soft, sheep-like, white breath.

        A beautiful bird
came to them
and said—

    UNATTAINABLE

Gentleman, Gentleman I

A T THE END OF AUGUST 1919, just before dawn, the guard, sober at last, jangling his bunch of keys, enters the solitary cell and leads Amedeo Modigliani, Italian painter, sculptor and vagabond, to the first of many cross-examinations.

In a fine, airy, sunny room he sees two very fine gentlemen. The first has a red nose and smells of wine, while the other looks like an apostle just descended from a cross.

Sit down, they say in unison.

The painter lowers himself onto a hard seat without a back.

They talk.

The gentleman with the red nose who drinks—

You have seen, then, that the world begins from below, that the world begins with breaking women's hymens, that the world in fact was born in hysterical virgins' blood.

And that consequently ART remains the eternal youth of the WORLD.

Yes, says the painter.

The gentleman who looks like an apostle just descended from a cross—

You have seen women in static and vulgar poses, with long necks and eyes without pupils, whose crooked bearing in fact EXPLAINS THE CROOKEDNESS OF GOD, the crookedness of His mercy, which is boundless, and the crookedness of man, His curious creation.

And you have seen that their yellow faces in fact represent sickness.

Yes, says the painter.

The gentleman with the red nose who drinks—

You have seen that LOVE IS FRIENDSHIP WITH A GENERALLY SAD END.

And you have seen that ART OVERCOMES DEPRESSION.

You've seen that too, haven't you?

Yes, says the painter.

The gentleman who looks like an apostle just descended from a cross—

You have seen that warm chromatic colours do not symbolise life, joy and happiness but rather failure, sickness, sorrow, sometimes even death.

You have seen that man is the measure of all things.

That a man's face is in fact a springboard for God.

Yes, says the painter.

The two gentlemen are angry.

They stand up at the same time and tie a black blindfold over his eyes.

You are free until tomorrow, they say in unison.

Some fifteen minutes later Amedeo Modigliani listens to the shuffling, uncertain steps of his guard, sober at last, behind him.

He hears the door scrape.

Then comes silence because he is alone again.

A Letter, Jeanne

H E WRITES THAT he is missing avenues of trees, friends, women, wine, Montparnasse by night or in rain, no matter.

He also mentions Nekrasov the Russian emigré, colours, and sharp, clearly defined afternoon shadows.

He is here, he is writing, very sadly because they often put a black blindfold over his eyes, as a punishment.

COLOUR—THAT IS MY LIFE, he adds at the end in unsteady handwriting. The letter ends—

JEANNE, LIFE, IT IS EITHER GLORY OR TUBERCULOSIS.

There is no third possibility.

He signs in the bottom right-hand corner of the crumpled paper.

In those long ostrich necks and on those faces which are drawn as they would be seen by someone with a squint or as we would see

them in a convex mirror, nothing allows us to sense the artist. Not the
drawing, nor psychological probing, and particularly not the colour.

ARTURO LANCELOTTI
Le Biennale del Dopoguerra Rome 1925

Modigliani was an aristocrat. His whole opus bears witness to
that. His canvases are full of nobility.

MAURICE DE VLAMINCK
Art Vivant Paris 1925

Painter, Butterfly

H IS BACK BENT, Amedeo Modigliani does not in fact notice, does not feel the butterfly's flight. Because he is dragging his heavy, fatal illness, dragging his bundle of cramped bones, dragging his sorrow, sickness and loneliness round his claustrophobic cell.

The insect is alive and impudent.

Brazen as the Bastille in 1879, like the chansons of Pan Zborowski, like the bark of a birch tree.

He remembers everything—

As though her face had remained for a few moments longer in his room frightening the phallusoid candles on the wall, frightening the stale, yellow, nicotine air.

And as though the dragon run through by Saint George's spear had burned his scrotum, his years (there were twenty-five of them), his brown, as yet unsold paintings.

And everything.

As though he had been jolted by the vault of an arched doorway, as though he had been bludgeoned by the Inquisition and as though he had died pinioned to a river bed.

Because the sweet whore Lolotte had left Amedeo.

Summer was nearly at an end.

The sun fell slantingly into the bleak cell.

The butterfly flitting around him was alive and impudent.

Brazen as the Bastille in 1879, like the chansons of Pan Zborowski, like the bark of a birch tree.

Liberty, Eyes

B UT HE did not kill it.

It is more likely that he recalled the false eyes on the butterfly's back and, still more important, its uncertain trajectory, only at first glance absurd, when the brazen insect flew into the wide open jaws of the drunken guard with his whole bunch of clanking keys in his helpless hands.

First it drenched the guard in bloody foam and only then did it die.

What a wonderful death, said Amedeo thinking of the butterfly. It is worth remembering that this significant day in the uncannily strange and brief life of Amedeo Modigliani passed in the following way—

—rising at six, from eight to nine he drove the sleep from his eyes with his thumb and forefinger, at nine yet another conversation with the two gentlemen and at ten o'clock liberty at last.

The first thing he wanted in the street was a cigarette.

After the gaoler left me I shined up my tin pannikin and studied my face in it. My expression was terribly serious, I thought, even when I tried to smile. I held the pannikin at different angles, but always my face had that same mournful, tense expression.

The sun was setting and it was the hour of which I'd rather not speak—'the nameless hour', I called it—when evening sounds were creeping up from all the floors of the prison in a sort of stealthy procession. I went to the barred window and in the last rays looked once again at my reflected face. It was as serious as before; and that wasn't surprising, as just then I was feeling serious. But, at the same time, I heard something that I hadn't heard for months. It was the sound of a voice; my own voice, there was no mistaking it. And I recognised it as the voice that for many a day of late had been buzzing in my ears. So I knew that all this time I'd been talking to myself.

ALBERT CAMUS   *The Outsider*

Gentleman, Gentleman II

THE GENTLEMAN with the red nose who drinks—
You have seen that human fear began even
before the demon.

You have seen that a poet's words do not sob out
of some lifeless invention, they spurt from moving,
passionate human mouths, like tongues of flame—
witnesses of the ruin of the world.

And you painted all that, did you?

Yes, says the painter.

The gentleman who looked like an apostle just
descended from a cross—

You have seen that the human comedy is just as
symbolic as tragedy. You have seen that people with
empty eyes cannot understand the sense of love, the
greatness of sacrifice or the extended hand of Divine
Providence, which prays, begs, says—

BELIEVE AND YOU WILL BE SAVED.

And you painted all that, did you?

Yes, says the painter.

The man with the red nose who drinks—

You have seen that light comes into being through the burning of destinies, that the face and its obverse exist, coexist, explain one another, like black and white, like truth and falsehood, like life and death, or such things. You have seen that the fine lie of human nakedness may signify aristocracy, that the prone body exposed to the eyes of strangers, however denuded, has preserved a kind of inner calm—the arrogance and elegance of a time that has passed.

And you painted all that, did you?

Yes, says the painter.

The gentlemen cross themselves, swear and spit at him.

Gabriel, Feathers

I N THE ROTONDE CAFÉ, Gabriel, an angel with no top to his head, waves his bedraggled wings to frighten the courtesans, the barman, the painters and drunks. Most of the customers are drunk and they applaud.

Ah, he's really good, squeals Jeanne, I'll piss myself laughing. Amedeo Modigliani, liberated and full of wine, stands up, puts his glass down and imitates a cockerel in front of the ladies.

The ladies giggle and fling up their legs.

Amedeo is now standing calmly, almost deathly rigid, talking.

Russians have blue eyes and Russians are sad. They are the midnight cranes of our drunken streets. Every day at half-past nine in the morning Nekrasov drinks tea and eats little shrimps from the sea.

His search is pointless.

We all know—

THE DEPTHS CANNOT BE REACHED.

Nekrasov, who is present, listens, lets Baronness Béatrice slip out of his arms, weeps and hugs everyone there. The Archangel Gabriel, who this time has come down to earth to take Modigliani's soul, slips on somebody's blood and, dragging a tablecloth over himself, falls onto the floor with a crash.

Consternation all around.

The ladies giggle and fling up their legs.

Gabriel does not get up, he looks at their legs.

Jeanne, Intimacy

I CAN TELL BY THE CROWS, says Jeanne. Her hands smell of tobacco, her lips of wine, her neck, spectral, long, straight, is as tasty as sour dough.

First the two of them lie, quite still, like icons, then his hand moves, quite slowly, onto her knee with which she is touching his thin ribs, fragile as piano keys.

He kisses her mouth and Jeanne stretches like a cat.

His forefinger touches her navel, then his hand moves over those first silken pussy hairs, soft and almost blonde, touching then the thick, warm juice of her open purple depths. It looks as though some mythical two-headed beast has stretched over the dirty, fairly low bed, hastily, greedily, thirstily breathing like a fish on dry land, sometimes emitting dreamlike, inhuman, throaty cries in the style—

"Aaahh", "no, no, noooo", "now, now" and the like.

Jeanne Hébuterne sighs and offers herself.

Take hold of my flanks, mumbles Amedeo Modigliani aware of his swollen, pulsing vein, and straddling his wife's soft body. She looks like all the

41

other naked beauties, alive, abandoned, devoted, as she touches his thighs with the soft down of her fingertips, as she touches his little purple head with her tongue, lips, mouth, as she moves her pelvis, arches her chest, as she breathes into his ear and finally accepts him, swinging her rear left-right-left-right-left-right.

Jeanne climaxes first and only then does Amedeo.

Soon afterwards, the pelican of dusk, a large voracious bird, swallows her long, almost saintly face, so that Amedeo Modigliani thinks for a moment, but only for a moment, not without horror, that he is lying in his grave, dying without farewell, becoming part of the soil, trees, water or a root, rock, no matter.

Jeanne puts on his shirt, three sizes too big for her, and goes over to the window. She is talking about autumn.

How do you mean autumn, the man asks uncertainly raising his satyr's head, is it not still summer according to the calendar.

No, it's autumn.

I can tell by the crows, says Jeanne.

Convex, Concave

THE MIRROR SEES for the last time a modest brown jacket, a thick grey scarf, a wall that is shabby, without decoration, and a chair with a rickety back, full of woodworm. He looks into his eyes and sees only sockets.

His arms drooping like cranes, pale, almost white, impotent, sick, hungry, weary. Touching his knee-cap with his left hand and with his right setting up, straight, broad, an untouched canvas, Amedeo Modigliani coughs and paints.

He looks into people's eyes and sees only sockets.

Jeanne Hébuterne, naked again now, having taken off the shirt that was three sizes too big for her, stepping unsteadily like a wounded calf, approaches the man and kisses the top of his head.

She looks into his eyes and sees only sockets.

Self-portrait, she asks.

Of course, he says.

Then she lies down, sleeps, and dreams of her one-year-old daughter Giovanna Modigliani. Meanwhile the man looks in the mirror and works.

Two hours later, everything becomes more difficult and darkness falls abruptly.

SELF-PORTRAIT. Oil on canvas, signature bottom right, São Paulo, Brazil, collection of Francisco Sobrinho Matarzo.

That self-portrait dated 1919, one of the artist's last works, is the finest and noblest expression of his art. Here he has presented himself without any enhancement, at a certain distance, but here too the nobility of his style lends nobility to his face, so that the words of his friend Max Jacob become clear to us—
' ... you have lived your great and simple life like an aristocrat.'

NELLO PONENTE

Friends, Parents

LEOPOLD AND HANKA ZBOROWSKI take the little girl—the one-year-old Giovanna Modigliani—home. They look at their reflections in puddles that are dirty, almost opaque. The child's eyes are open, dark, longing for sun. The adults talk euphorically, gaily, occasionally taking a drink from a bright bottle that looks as though the sun had entered it.

They see the drunken Cocteau in front of the Rotonde, raving, reciting Dante, his own poems, and other great saints.

Hello, they say.

Hello, says Cocteau.

At the end of another road Zborowski buys opium from an Arab.

They continue walking, eerily happy that their friend has been freed.

They sing.

They step firmly through the streets and the child walks behind them.

Knives, Pearls

THAT IS HOW they come to Madame Carmelita. The opium begins to work from below.

First it transforms the heads of their women into balloons, and then their eyes into bright, midsummer fireflies. THEY KNOW THE SECRET says Amedeo Modigliani drunkenly and afterwards he smokes, drying the incomplete face on the easel with his breath.

BALTHAZAR, CASPAR, MELCHIOR, gabbles the Pole with crazily bristling hair, the poet and merchant Pan Leopold Zborowski.

The three holy kings, says Hanka.

Five minutes later, armed with knives, the men go down to the floor below, they whisper and then they bang on the door.

They return significantly more quietly, having disfigured with their blades the face, body and womb of Madame Carmelita. Scattering the pearls.

That's how pigs end up, declares Zborowski.

They sit down on the floor, open champagne and drink, with their wives, late into the night. At half-past nine in the evening, they carry the sleeping child into the other room, and at half-past eleven cold visits them, riding in on a tail of marijuana, icing the windows, human breath, women's laughter and the memory of early spring that will never come again.

The most propitious hour, says Leopold Zborowski then, is the one between one and two, because that is when the malevolent have no power. Cold comes late at night when a person is sleeping, because all those who are tormented by insomnia, tormented by the curse of wakefulness, then come face to face with the malevolent—helpless, guilty without real guilt.

Marked like all witnesses.

Then Zborowski suddenly falls silent, gulping from the bottle big, sad, emigré mouthfuls of tart wine from Avignon.

The others are either drunk or they clink glasses.

Sleep and peace do not come.

What is insomnia?
The question is rhetorical. I know the answer only too well.

It is to count off and dread in the small hours the fateful harsh strokes of the chime. It is attempting with ineffectual magic to breathe smoothly. It is the burden of a body that abruptly shifts sides. It is shutting the eyelids down tight. It is a state like fever and is assuredly not watchfulness. It is saying over bits of paragraphs read years and years before. It is knowing how guilty you are to be lying awake when others are asleep. It is trying to sink into slumber and being unable to sink into slumber. It is the horror of being and going on being. It is the dubious daybreak.

JORGE LUIS BORGES   *Two Types of Insomnia*

Morning, Milk

THE NEXT MORNING Mr Balthazar, the milkman, finds the dead sow-woman filled with pearls.

MY GOD, says Balthazar, and looks at the hungry children.

The children do not cry, they do not run away, nor do they pray to God.

They are silent.

Morning, Hunger

I N THE MORNING, of course, they are all aware of the collective hallucination of the previous night. Hanka and Jeanne prepare breakfast, the men smoke and talk about Cézanne, Toulouse-Lautrec, and the loveliness of the elongated form in African statuettes.

They also talk about death.

They even mention Madame Carmelita, the land-lady with the three-tier stomach, and her sad, ugly end, when she expired, grunting like a small sow, suffocated by heaps and heaps of round pearls. They eat their breakfast greedily and, with his mouth full, Amedeo Modigliani talks about his dream of the previous night, about the hallucinatory, almost real knives that gleamed in the darkness of the stuffy staircase. About warm blood and about the cold, neon sheen of the pearls in her insides.

In the end they all agree that this death and this kind of death have PROFOUND MEANING.

In the nineteen-fifties, in her book, *Modigliani—Man and Myth*, Jeanne Modigliani described this event as a DREAM OF DREAMS, A SONG OF SONGS, as the complete triumph of the imagination over banal reality. One needs only to dream, she writes, one needs only to want something really, sincerely, strongly, with one's whole being and DREAM WILL BECOME REALITY.

AND REALITY IS NOTHING OTHER THAN YET ANOTHER DREAM.

And so on multiplied and intertwined into infinity. As in a room with a thousand mirrors.

The chapter ends with the words:

YOU REALLY WERE A GREAT MAN.

FATHER.

Béatrice, Dante

T HE SECOND PART of our story of the uncannily strange and brief life of Amedeo Modigliani, painter, bohemian and vagabond, begins one warm October day in 1919, in the well-known Parisian bar La Rotonde, where we find three people, Amedeo Modigliani, Jean Cocteau and Baroness Béatrice, gathered round a table covered with sketches and papers, loudly discussing something, slicing their hands decisively through the lazy blue nicotine smoke. Three tables further away, behind them, we see a man cutting lines of verse with a narrow child's knife into the heavy old wooden case of his favourite guitar. The name of that man is Max Jacob.

In the dusk of that same day the bar-setting is the same, but the actor-customers are arranged like this:

Baroness Béatrice and Modigliani are sitting at a table together, and a man, completely red in the face, partly with wine, partly because of the very distinct proximity of a slender girl in blue, is whispering in her ear some sort of words, which make her lips part like a leech into a sincere smile. Later some other people join them at their table, they drink champagne, something is evidently being celebrated, and, after closing time, in the street, the drunken Amedeo Modigliani recites extracts from Dante's *Divine Comedy*, and then falls into the arms of the woman, Baroness Béatrice, who leads him to her airy, orderly and—remarkable!—spacious apartment. She puts him into bed, the man's teeth chatter and he shivers, and in the end she covers him with her own body.

Doe, Intimacy

A S SHE CARESSED his sleepy, drooping head, settled sweetly on her bare breasts, running the index finger of her left hand over his dark brow, Baroness Béatrice, somewhat to her surprise, felt his third eye. The pupil of that eye was turned inwards, into his head, and cautiously, like a cat approaching a piece of bacon—not to waken the man—the woman brought the fig of her lips to his sleeping brow, stretched her hand along the keyboard of his ribs, circling round his navel, and finally settling in the warm nest between his legs. Her quickened breathing, but more her downy touch, excited and woke Modigliani, who opened his eyes and shivered, at which Baroness Béatrice, shyly as a doe, withdrew her hand and somewhat foolishly, like a child caught stealing jam from a high shelf, smiled into the darkness.

Paris, Fog

W RAPPED IN FOG, dense and bad like cheese, Paris had withdrawn from its squares, and lay sleepily silent, yawning. Some people were performing a play by Molière on the Place du Trocadéro with an enthusiasm rarely seen.

The greasy October day, all that fog that had become the final point, the source of all the light, in any case meagre, and all the sounds, in any case muffled, made the actors' movements somehow exalted, divine.

It seemed as though those people who were rapidly reciting sentences, mixing French and Italian words, had come to this Paris square from nowhere, like ghosts from some quite different age, almost forgotten, in which women smelled of sin and men of good wines, strong tobacco and Sunday afternoons spent hunting.

The audience of this heavenly performance by travelling players was extremely modest, consisting of a few tramps and our painter Amedeo Modigliani, who lit one cigarette after another, gazing lengthily, dully, as though hypnotised, at the soft movements in the fog.

Some kind of comedy, the painter asked the man beside him.

No idea.

Maybe something free at last, replied a tramp.

Amedeo Modigliani went on standing there for a while longer, coughing, the wind piercing his temples, and then finally turned away and let his feet carry him of their own accord to Montparnasse.

Apples, Wine

THIS INCIDENT also occurred in Paris, in 1919, and according to Amedeo's daughter Giovanna Modigliani, who heard about it first-hand and recorded it in her book, *Modigliani—Man and Myth*, it happened like this:

At some stage in the autumn of the said year, the French-Italian painter Amedeo Modigliani, following his old—he would say also good—custom, called in the early hours of one morning into the Rotonde café for a morning coffee and a drink.

"YES?" said the bad-tempered barman to the new arrival who had just sat down at the bar. "APPLES AND WINE," replied Modigliani.

"BUT, SIR," said the barman surprised, "WE DON'T SERVE APPLES!"

"WHAT CAN WE DO," Modigliani is supposed to have responded sadly, "IF THERE'S NO RAIN, ICE IS GOOD. SO GIVE ME JUST WINE ... "

Jeanne, Motherhood I

THE LIGHT, coming in misty cascades from the street transforms her naked, sleepy body, languid with sleep, into an arabesque. Her face is a dappled African mask.

Jeanne breathes evenly.

Inhalation.

Exhalation.

Her hair, heavy, red as a flame, is strewn over the pillows.

Touched by the sight of his sleeping wife, Jeanne Hébuterne, Amedeo Modigliani approaches, quietly as though he was truly a shadow, and places his ear on her belly, just slightly taut with motherhood.

Warm, infinite.

Amedeo Modigliani hears inside, within her, a third heart beating.

Dream, Kandinsky

WHILE HE NIBBLED the leaves of a vine, like a tame rabbit that returns to the garden before each winter.

While he breathed in the scent of her sticky hair through the darkness.

While he dreamed that he was awake, but still dreaming.

While he hushed the wind in her nostrils.

While he said the rosary of her name,

mechanically, persistently and slowly.

Jeanne was a boy.

Jeanne was a shepherd.

While he pressed sleep into her eyebrows and eyelashes with the thumb and forefinger of his left hand.

While he made castanets of her knees.

While he kissed with the fig of his lips the silver chain round her neck with a medallion of Our Lady of Livorno.

While he touched with the feathers of a nameless bird the spring nest of her—and his—motherhood.

While it seemed to him in his delusion that he had been born anew.

While he cleaned the dust of angels out from under her nails and from her fingers.

While he said the rosary of her name,
mechanically, persistently and slowly.
The Blue Rider
came to them
and said:
UNATTAINABLE.

Renoir, Star

IN THE GRIP of the December night of the third day of December, 1919—the day that the weary painter Renoir died—Amedeo Modigliani, the 'little Jew from Livorno', as his contemporaries called him, alone in his studio, is drawing with a black pencil, in broad, expansive strokes the long, pale face of a tender old woman, Eugénie Garsin-Modigliani, his mother.

On the table, beside the portfolio of sketches, stands a bottle of wine, just begun.

Outside, it is freezing.

The Rue de la Grande Chaumière puts on a winter shirt out of ancient tales and fairy-stories.

The painter coughs.

He can feel his beard, the last of his life, growing suddenly as though it were spring grass.

Modigliani lays down his pencil, and completely inaudibly, as though he is no longer an inhabitant of this world, as though he has already passed over into the world of memories and shadows, he approaches his bed and, with a deep sigh, fully dressed, he lies down.

At the moment when his breathing becomes a steady, tranquil sibilance, a single star, the brightest, breaks out of the sky above Paris and falls.

Renoir.

Modigliani lived in a heroic age. He suffered its counterblows. From the outset, all his canvases bear the mark of the profound disquiet ·that troubled the best of his contemporaries.

Modigliani was too great an artist to remain outside the ardent throng. But his specific style was never altered by a fashion that was strange.

WALDEMAR GEORGES

68

Paris, Dada

I N THE COURSE of his uncannily strange and brief
life, Amedeo Modigliani, painter, bohemian and
vagabond, had three encounters with Monsieur
Charles-Édouard Jeanneret, known as Le Corbusier.

A first time, just one time, and the last time.

They met by chance, in the street.

Amedeo Modigliani was roaming the streets, clutch-
ing a terrifying emptiness in his pockets, while the
wind of oblivion wound through his uncombed hair
and beard, a wind that confuses human thoughts,
interweaves sleep and desires, merges two worlds,
that of the everyday and the one that is rarely, almost
never, reached by human perception or experience.

The Second Kingdom of Death.

When he first caught sight of the figure of Charles-
Édouard Jeanneret, also known as Le Corbusier,
dressed in a white suit and a red hat, on which a bird,
a dodo, was sleeping, Modigliani felt that he had seen
the Angel of Dadaism.

Everything confirmed it.

Le Corbusier's cane made of ivory, his moustache pointed upwards like the hands of a clock indicating ten minutes past ten (\/), but, above all, his curious, somehow square smile whose shape contained something of the reduction, simplicity, perfection of a cube or a dice.

Hello bird, said Le Corbusier.

Amedeo Modigliani smiled and touched the rim of his shabby hat with his forefinger.

Farewell earth, farewell water.

Farewell dead dodo bird, Modigliani joked.

Le Corbusier, whose glance was so swift that he was able to see his own back, took four dice out of the left-hand inside pocket of his jacket, offered them to Modigliani, turned and disappeared into the crowd. Instead of numbers, there were four letters engraved on them.

D—A—D—A, read Modigliani.

Then he coughed huskily, painfully, and continued his vain, aimless walk without end.

Life is a dream which cannot be understood while it is being dreamed, thought the painter as the day, in any case already dead, was transformed into yet another weighty, cold night of fasting.

Circus, Silence

THE FOLLOWING DAY he got drunk with Soutine. They drank wine at the Rotonde, like thirsty soldiers, alone, each absorbed in his own silence, until their eyes became poppy flowers, and their nose and ears as loud as a waterfall.

Today is Friday, said Soutine as they emerged into the meagre light of Montparnasse, holding onto the left-hand sleeve of his great friend's jacket.

There was no reply.

Silence from the other side.

An inexplicable, empty, vast silence had settled in Amedeo Modigliani.

Their red faces, just a little sprinkled with perspiration, seemed to have slipped off a poster for the circus that often came in the festive colourful days leading up to Christmas, to the little place in the south where the painter spent his childhood.

They walked.

Together, but nevertheless each for himself, separately.

And each of them, Modigliani and Soutine, trying to shout louder than his own silence.

Once he'd gone, I felt calm again. But all this excitement had exhausted me and I dropped heavily on to my sleeping-plank. I must have had a longish sleep, for, when I woke, the stars were shining down on my face. Sounds of the countryside came faintly in, and the cool night air, veined with smells of earth and salt, fanned my cheeks. The marvellous peace of the sleepbound summer night flooded through me like a tide. Then, just on the edge of daybreak, I heard a steamer's siren. People were starting on a voyage to a world which had ceased to concern me, for ever. Almost for the first time in many months I thought of my mother. And now, it seemed to me, I understood why at her life's end she had taken on a 'fiancé'; why she'd played at making a fresh start. There, too, in that Home where lives were flickering out, the dusk came as a mournful solace. With death so near, Mother must have felt like someone on the brink of freedom, ready to start life all over again. No one, no one in the world had any right to weep for her. And I, too, felt ready to start life over again. It was as if that great rush of anger had washed me clean, emptied me of hope, and, gazing up at the dark sky spangled with its signs and stars, for the first time, the first, I laid my heart open to the benign indifference of the universe. To feel it so like myself, indeed so brotherly, made me realize that I'd been happy, and that I was happy still. For all to be accomplished, for me to feel less lonely, all that remained was to hope that on the day of my execution there should be a huge crowd of spectators and that they should greet me with howls of execration.

ALBERT CAMUS, *The Outsider*

Montparnasse, Night

"INTO A NEW YEAR. Into a new life!" That is what was written on the postcard that the painter Amedeo Modigliani received from his old childhood friend Oscar M to greet the New Year 1920.

Festive fever.

The whole city was waiting for the little God to be born again in the straw. The streets were already echoing with firecrackers, the laughter of the sated, drunk and contented, the future had already arrived—in the twentieth year of the twentieth century, it seemed that a new golden age was beginning for the whole of humanity.

In the Rue de la Grande Chaumière, in the Modiglianis' modest flat, the adults were swallowing the holy smoke that comes from strange oriental pipes while the child, Giovanna, her eyes the colour of extinguished ash, was looking out of the window, down the street, suppressing the little frozen dove of her anxiety, simply staring as she waited for the white reindeers and sled of Saint Nicholas the Gift-Giver.

The world is full of scoundrels, the world has always been full of scoundrels, whispered Amedeo Modigliani, as though he were saying a prayer, while the beard on his face changed colour and turned to silver.

The world is full of scoundrels. Jeanne Hébuterne, whose hair reminded him increasingly of the colour of the poppies in Livorno, sprinkled her sorrow through the room like water, it seemed that, with the help of an inner eye, this noble woman could already see two new graves, one beside the other, under the fresh snow, weather when no one leaves the house, in the Père Lachaise cemetery in Paris.

The wise thing is to pluck out one's heart in good time, he says.

Before sorrow settles in it.

She gets up from the worm-eaten chair, goes up to the man and places her left hand on the seemingly still boyish crown of his head.

Amedeo Modigliani turns his head and sinks his face into warm silk.

The child has fallen asleep on the floor.

The story of Saint Nicholas and the gifts—the first great lie in the life of Giovanna Modigliani.

Although she waited a long, long, long time with big wishes concealed in her small heart—he did not appear.

The Rue de la Grande Chaumière remained empty.

The world is full of scoundrels.

Jeanne, Motherhood II

J EANNE IS STILL the bud of a winter rose, frozen and iron-bound, her advanced pregnancy makes her face even more beautiful, nobler, but ailing Amedeo Modigliani can already see quite clearly through his eyes, red-hot with fever, that some kind of immeasurable and incalculable sorrow is blossoming in her. The strange docility and gentleness of this fettered doe, soft with the new life swelling inside her, makes the sick man still more unhappy, bewildered, erratic.

The weather appears to be changing, says Jeanne as they lie together in the dark, their limbs intertwined, the sky will soon be entering the constellation of Cancer.

Of course, says Modigliani.

Bad times are coming because the world is full of scoundrels.

Sleep eludes him and the man gets up, goes over to the easel and gazes for a long time at the untouched and empty white canvas.

He sighs, goes to the window and throws it wide open.

Outside something smells wet and terrible, it smells of poverty and rain-soaked dogs, of a journey with no home-coming, of requiems and dirges, it smells of the chill from beyond the grave, and the painter Amedeo Modigliani knows that it is snow.

Montparnasse, Snow

FINALLY, ON THE TWENTY-FIFTH of December 1920 AD, on Christmas Day, it snowed.

A heavy wet shawl covered the earth.

Amedeo Modigliani is holding in his hand a summons to a court hearing in connection with the death of the sow-woman Carmelita. Her sister, Donna Clara, has already crossed the frontier.

Alone in the street.

He breathes with difficulty.

The painter Amedeo Modigliani is weary.

There is no point in movement, he thinks, he spreads his arms and turns his face towards the sky, which sends down its ghastly feathers.

It's a bird, it seems to him, but his breath is getting shorter, stopping altogether, the man staggers, he is near the end, and finally, entirely resigned, Amedeo Modigliani buries his face in the frozen silk.

Happy Christmas, sorrowful bird, says his friend Chaim Soutine some icy minutes later, lifting him from the white, festive and ghostly pavement of Montparnasse.

From somewhere, in the distance, church bells with their galvanised clattering, invite the faithful to mass.

Leopold, Béatrice

IN PARIS, at the beginning of January 1920, Leopold Zborowski, an antiquarian from Poland, offered Baronness Béatrice six nudes by Amedeo Modigliani in small quarto format.

The Baronness bought them and when they were delivered to her she exchanged a few words with him.

The Pole used some of the money to buy wine and fish.

He drank the rest.

In March, the second day of spring in that same year, the Baronness learned from a passenger on the Hypnos that in the night between the twenty-fourth and twenty-fifth of January, in the paupers' Hôpital de la Charité, Amedeo Modigliani had given up his consumption-tormented soul.

He was buried soon afterwards.

HE HAD A BIG HEART wrote Baronness Béatrice in her diary, hiccuping tipsily, that same evening, squinting over the scant, niggardly, flickering yellow light of her candle.

In the morning she gave her still youthful body to the captain.

Absurd is the man who, out of a fundamental absurdity, draws, without hesitation, conclusions that impose themselves. There is the same displacement of sense as when young people dancing 'swing' are called swing. So what is the absurd as primary state, as original given? Nothing less than the relation of man to the world. Primal absurdity manifests above all a divorce: the divorce between the aspirations of man towards unity and the insurmountable dualism of the spirit and of nature, between the striving of man for the eternal and the finite character of his existence, between the 'concern' that is his very essence and the vanity of his efforts. Death, the irreducible pluralism of truths and beings, the unintelligibility of the real, chance, those are the poles of the absurd.

JEAN-PAUL SARTRE,
Analysis of *The Outsider*

Giovanna, Emigrés

As far as I know, Giovanna Modigliani told three bearded Poles in Florence in 1958, my father's troubles began on Twelfth Night 1920 when, in the Rotonde café, he sold the Archangel Gabriel the last fragment of his lungs that were in any case ruined.

With some of the money my father bought wine and fish.

He drank the rest.

He came home blind drunk and coughed up blood for days.

By the end of the month he was dead.

And that was about it.

Giovanna Modigliani then drank the rest of her coffee and went out into the sweltering crowd in the street. What a holy misfortune, said the first Pole, who reeked of vodka, to bear the name of Modigliani all one's life.

Of course, said the others.

They clinked their glasses and drank.

Amedeo, Angel I

LOLOTTE, THE ACACIA of the Paris underworld, bright as a ray of sunshine, stepping gaily as though she were dancing a polka, like a music-hall queen, the heels of her shoes barely touching the pavement in front of the Rotonde, approaches a tall thin man and kisses him on the top of his head.

Who are you waiting for, sailor, she says.

Mmmm, it smells of roses here, the painter barely murmurs.

Lolotte looks him in the eye and notices that he is blind drunk.

I feel, she says later in a hotel room, lying on her side like a Venus, I feel you with my face, hands, breasts and I see, I see the proximity, the dangerous proximity of the yellow colour of DEATH. On the sky beneath the arc of the moon, on your face, under the vault of your eyebrows, in the street, under the streetlights, and everywhere, everywhere, everywhere.

In your paintings, Modigliani.

Everywhere, everywhere is the yellow furrow of death.

I am afraid for you, sailor.

The man says nothing and turns onto his other side with a sigh.

He stares dully into the darkness.

Lolotte straightens up, lights a cigarette and lets her tears fall down her face.

The spring comes quietly, says the painter, wiping away her tears, spring awakens all things, touches my hair, my hand, it enters my dreams.

Spring Comes Quietly.

THESE SENTIMENTAL WORDS, almost stupid, but still so tender, remind Lolotte of her childhood, of her grandmother's soft hands, white as a down quilt, of that time without men, alcohol or tuberculosis.

Of the time when she was still Mother's blonde angel.

They remind her of her hymen, virgo intacta, of her father's moustache, her mother's cooking and all that dissipated time, vanished forever.

And then the Angel of Sleep, a strange bird without feathers, comes down from the proud towers of the church and covers her eyes with his wing.

The painter breathes tensely and discordantly in the darkness and feels for her breasts with his stiff fingers.

He thinks how innocent and blind her nipples are.

Amedeo, Angel II

O N THE SIXTH OF JANUARY 1920 AD, on the Feast of the Three Kings, looking vaguely at the stains on the bar, Gabriel, the angel without a top to his head, turning his hands towards the heavens, drunk, tired, sick, drugged, belching, bought from Amedeo Modigliani a slimy, bloody, festering piece of meat for a modest handful of tattered banknotes.

Somewhere in the middle of the nineteen-fifties Giovanna Modigliani, Amedeo's daughter, in her book, *Modigliani—Man and Myth*, described this commercial enterprise like this:

"As far as I know, she writes, my father's troubles began on Twelfth Night 1920 when, in the Rotonde café he sold the Archangel Gabriel the last fragment of his lungs that were in any case ruined.

With some of the money my father bought wine and fish.

He drank the rest.

He came home blind drunk and vomited blood for days.

91

By the end of the month he was dead.

And that was about it."

The vague and blurred memories of a woman (a child at the time), Cocteau's note from 1923, the half-stammered statement of Monsieur Michel who had that morning taken refuge in the Rotonde from the onslaughts of the North Star and finally a newspaper article signed with the initials M J (Max Jacob) which referred to an unusual pact between a man and an angel, about the purchase of a lung and the yellow face of Amedeo Modigliani, Italian painter and sculptor, were the only proof of this hideous, lunatic, fatal DRUNKEN GAME.

Soon after that (more precisely thirteen days later), the life course of Amedeo Modigliani came to an end in a cheap little room in the paupers' Hôpital de la Charité. And the day after his death, Jeanne Hébuterne, his wife, threw herself out of the window of her parents' house.

They say that she was in the eighth month of pregnancy.

Amedeo and Béatrice

IN HER ROOM that smells of ether oil, with her hair filled with the feathers of large white birds, her eyelids still heavy as the breath of angels, Baronness Béatrice consumes a light breakfast followed by tart, sour red wine from Avignon. It's like drinking mint, thinks Béatrice, rubbing her eyes sleepily.

We see Amedeo Modigliani, tormented by frequent and demanding police hearings (in connection with the death of Madame Carmelita), alcoholism and tuberculosis, shivering like a drenched cockerel, outside the Baronness's door, holding under his arm a middle-sized picture of the pretty face of the little harlot Lolotte. He presses the doorbell and starts to wait with the patience characteristic only of the desperate. The widow of Prince Stanislawksi, patroness of the arts, occasional lover of Lautrec, a secret talented poet, inexplicably long and unhappily in love with Nekrasov the Russian emigré and drunkard, nymphomaniac, Catholic

93

and lover of wine, Baronness Béatrice opens the heavy baroque door, smiles, speaks, and takes hold of the painter's arm.

In the hallway she leans her full round breasts against the man's emaciated torso.

I hope, she says, that there is a difference between Adam the weary hunter and the furious deceiver, idler, drunkard and buffoon dissolute Eros. Because only leisure, only that fine patina of everyday boredom, can create art. Great, sad and inaccessible ART.

THE FUTURE BELONGS TO THE MISUNDERSTOOD.

HOMO FABER DOES NOT DREAM.

He has long ago lost all hope in life.

As she says this, Béatrice slowly opens the man's fly and inserts her long, gold-encumbered fingers into his trousers. She breathes into his ear.

She leads him to her bedroom.

Everything smells of ether oil, the room is spacious, white, clean.

Soon they are naked.

And then Béatrice moves her motherly vulva towards his problematic manhood.

The face of Amedeo Modigliani flushes with a pink glow.

Perhaps for the last time.

And then for a long while after making love they drink wine, talk about colours, brushes, canvases, in a word they bore themselves.

The afternoon, which comes quietly, from the tips of the bare trees, finds them asleep.

Amedeo, Trial I

I T HAPPENS IN PARIS, the ninth of January 1920 AD.
The cold weather has kept people riveted to
their homes, so that in the chilly courtroom we no-
tice only a few individuals. Among them, Jeanne
Hébuterne stands out with her flaming red hair.
Leopold Zborowski is not present.

Some time in February 1926, the judge, Monsieur
Bertalanffy, with the face of a hardened gastritis-
sufferer, was to tell Baronness Béatrice, in the
Rotonde, having swallowed his bicarbonate of soda,
the scandalous story of the uncanny behaviour of
Amedeo Modigliani during the trial in connection
with the death of Madame Carmelita.

In her intimate diary, under a date which we
assume is accurate, Baronness Béatrice wrote a
poem which Jeanne Modigliani published in full,
in the middle of the nineteen-fifties, in her book
Modigliani—Man and Myth.

The poem is elegiac, filled with hints of its au-
thor's imminently approaching death and quite good

97

descriptions of the landscape of her native Poland, ravaged by plague, hunger and war.

Jeanne Modigliani presumes that this poem was the last that the already slightly deranged noblewoman wrote before all trace of her was lost somewhere on the Russian border, in the winter of 1943.

And as for Amedeo Modigliani's scandalous behaviour on the occasion of the trial, in her book Jeanne Modigliani mentions only that her father danced the whole time, his arms spread like Christ, quoting Dante and from time to time opening his fly.

Acquitted for lack of evidence, she writes at the end of the chapter.

Clara, Candles

DONNA CLARA, daughter of Puerto Rico, third sister of the sow-woman Carmelita, came to Paris barefoot, carrying with her a painting of three saints spitting

—the first was Saint Sylvester

—the second John the Baptist

—and the third Saint Paul, God of Fish and King of Ravens.

She arrived the night after Epiphany, drunk and tired, barefoot, black as the very depths of night, with the face of Saint Theresa in ecstasy.

Closing the heavy lead door, Donna Clara noticed on the wall yellow, phallusoid, extravagant candles.

MON DIEU, she thought, this is the work of an Angel.

And then she turned her lovely, black face towards the crucifix and began to pray in a murmur.

Quietly, as though she was afraid of something.

Amedeo, Clara

AFTER THE THIRD LITRE of wine, they are already naked and he is kissing her. Clara has the taut stomach of a bitch, sharp elbows and the long, thin legs of hungry Puerto Rican boys.

And then, because a harlot and a saint are separated only by one almost insignificant step, we see Donna Clara kneeling and using her mouth to work on the painter's elongated, crooked member.

They climax at almost the same time, jerkily, in spasms.

The painter's legs give out completely and with a loud, almost painful, cry, he collapses onto the floor, across the woman.

Her black face is white with his semen.

As he lies, the man plays with her breasts and the little, probably gold, crucifix between them.

They tell each other their names, introduce one another, that is, and go on smiling at each other for a long time in the darkness. Afterwards they rest and sleep.

Because in the end the fine, almost golden, dust of sleep settled on their eyes.

Fear, Dream III

A GRAVEYARD WHERE SAINT PAUL drags out of the pregnant woman with his bare and unclean hands a newborn calf with candles instead of horns.

A graveyard where black and white dolphins are breakfasting on the huge babbling tongues of Puerto Rican mothers, nuns and prostitutes.

A graveyard where orchids have the face of a mother.

A graveyard where a strong southerly wind strips the skin from bones.

Simply, a graveyard.

A graveyard that explains itself by death.

He wakes with moist temples, shivering, terrified, and tells the woman his dream. She turns onto her other side and says nothing.

Jesus, he says to her then, does this dream mean the dangerous proximity of death. Donna Clara, still naked, gets up, makes them tea and as she does so explains in detail the symbols of the dream.

Finally she says: still, it is better than dreaming about a snake.

What a singular, attractive figure is Modigliani! In a life as disoriented as could be, this painter-sculptor and sculptor-painter was able to create wonderful nudes and no less exceptional portraits.

ADOLPHE BASLER

Paris, Spawning Ground

Leaving donna clara asleep and alone, Amedeo Modigliani went out into the dirty, cramped, dank streets of Montparnasse. He smoked, looking at the expressionless faces of the little girl prostitutes. He thought of Lolotte, the blue flamingo.

In the Rotonde, over their third litre of wine, Leopold Zborowski told him about the raspberry smell of his wife's thighs, about himself, drugs, wine, about Paris which was, curiously enough, a TAROT-TOWN, that is just what he said: TAROT-TOWN.

Don't ask, my friend, said Zborowski drunkenly, why darkness falls and why water falls on the TAROT-TOWN.

I used to love standing alone, holding a flag in the wind, he went on.

I loved imitating an orchid, a bottle of wine and Dante.

I loved teaching deer, nuns or painters.

And then solitude mounted me,

and then silence mounted me,

and then poverty mounted me.

But my horse was not strong enough.

But my horse is an ordinary nag.

The cards are badly dealt.

The ones I have in my hands are significantly weaker than the ones in the hands of my opponents.

ECCE HOMO—they cry because this TAROT is being played with living people.

ECCE HOMO—they cry because they know that they have better trumps.

ECCE HOMO—they cry because they know that they always, simply always, win.

And then solitude mounted me,

and then silence mounted me,

and then poverty mounted me.

But my horse was not strong enough.

But my horse is an ordinary nag.

And that is why never ask me, my friend, Zborowski ended his angelic ravings, hiccuping, why darkness falls and why water falls on the TAROT-TOWN.

Don't ever ask.

Full-stop.

The street met them like two crawling, lecherous crabs, like two dumb carp which, with glassy eyes, fell dully, stupidly, noiselessly into the opening of a sewer.

WHAT A CHEAP END, thought Amedeo Modigliani, aware of the stench of human excrement and urine all over him.

Amedeo, Rats

NEKRASOV FOUND THEM and woke them.
Removing the fattened rats from their lapels, Nekrasov, a tall and tubercular Russian émigré, warmed their frozen hands, ears, palms, lips, with his breath.

Where is that woman, whispered Modigliani, whom I kissed on the breasts and three spans lower down. Where is she who waits for my loving charity with the wisdom of a Mandarin. Where, where, oh where is my dear Jeanne Hébuterne.

Nekrasov told the story later on: As I lifted him up, I felt Amedeo's downy, hazy, almost fluid incorporality; I heard his rasping breath, his nebulous talk of Jeanne Hébuterne; I noticed on his thin, elongated neck, almost like that of a crane, the yellow flower of madness, irregular, newly formed. Putting him down for a moment in order to pick Zborowski up out of the sewer as well (he was drunker and heavier) I was aware of a soft breeze on my neck, warm and barely audible, like the wing-beat of a humming-bird. I turned round, Nekrasov continued, and saw Amedeo float up and place his pale hand, almost white as a streak of light, on the proud towers of the church. Rats fell from him like ripe pears.

Amedeo, Trial II

IT HAPPENED IN PARIS, early on the morning of the nineteenth of January 1920 AD, when, in the unaired, cold, stale courtroom, Amedeo Modigliani, as the first accused in the affair of Madame Carmelita, stood before the astonished, honourable judge, imitating a cockerel and reciting Dante in the original, holding his fly with his left hand the whole time.

Hoarse, suffering from a cold, tormented by gastritis, the investigating judge Monsieur Bertalanffy accepted that his investigation was in a blind alley, asked Zborowski routine questions, coughed, filled and emptied his pipe, and finally put the whole case on file.

Amedeo Modigliani, now entirely incorporeal, without lungs, without pupils, feverishly celebrated his freedom, draining glasses of red wine in long, elephantine gulps. In a café Jeanne Hébuterne, his wife, broke a glass and then ate it.

Later Zborowski came as well, bringing the icy tentacles of winter in with him.

They shook hands.

They talked.

Finally Leopold Zborowski mentioned pigs, pearls and the spring that would not come.

He wept, waiting for his wife Hanka.

Amedeo, Pathos

DONNA CLARA, the painter told her, coughing drily, all unhappy women have small breasts. Everything comes to an end where fury and impotence begin. Oblivion is:

total indifference in the face of death,

which is a pure, large, white ball,

IT'S SNOWING, said Donna Clara, freeing her neck from his embrace. Large, grainy, sickly snowflakes were falling. Wet is sorrow and sorrow is wet.

and its hand, the painter told her, coughing drily, its hand approached me as I slept and touched my chest, nails, hair. Its dangerous proximity was no more than three spans from me. A large dead army of smiling storks is marching on my cheek, Clara. Drunken friends dragged me out of hell.

There, for a whole six months, one's hands are raised to the sky. The apples, roses and tender wilting primroses of your dead spring.

Clara, we are leaving,

this time, for instance, with the wind.

In my sleep last night I was on the edge of delirium, I wept, smiling at the grave of your joints. And the beautiful birds, the beautiful birds of our years were escaping, stupidly, seasonally, from the sky, leaving it empty. And the beautiful birds were losing their feathers.

Clara, we are leaving,

foolishly like this, recklessly, if only it's not too late.

Because nothing can bring back that moment between an exhalation and the next inhalation, that moment when a man is closest to death. I was born in 1884 and I died last summer.

This now, I think, is only a dream.

It is horrible in the street.

The room is empty, literally empty, and I feel the icy terror of Montparnasse at night. The last drunks are vainly searching for the big strange bird: THE ANGEL OF SLEEP.

Little coloured boxes, says Donna Clara, kissing his fingers, tender as the wings of mosquitoes, transparent. Little coloured boxes borne by water. In which poets lie buried. Dead, quite dead, abandoned to the current.

Because we certainly have no use for living poets.

I remember everything, the painter tells her, coughing drily, the summer arrived on yellow lanterns, on the tail of a dragonfly, on the backsides of grasshoppers, like withered peaches touching the very DEPTHS OF LIFE with their brittle bodies—I have ceased to exist.

Clara, I have fallen.

As I talked about my sleepy nudes, yellow, ugly, singed pain, crouching in my alveolas and bronchioles, knocking lengthily, insidiously, growing tenaciously like roots, ramifying, spreading, growing.

Clara, I have fallen.

Entwined like a spider and a fly, says Donna Clara, running her hand over his emaciated torso, like a spider and a fly we are entwined in a vortex of love and death. The fly inevitably dies because it was not wise, while the spider lives on, because it had the patience to wait and because it was stronger.

Amedeo Modigliani smiles weakly, they stop talking abruptly, and naked as they are they melt into one another. As they make love the woman closes her eyes because his face frightens her.

Amedeo, Children

C HILDREN IN THE PARK, by the monument,
are collecting pigeon droppings, with joyful
squeals. Thinking, probably, that they are glass, or
God forbid, pearls.

Amedeo Modigliani shudders, coughs, and leaves
them to it. He has four more days to live and does
not care whether someone cannot tell the difference
between shit and pearls.

Cocteau, A Walk

LEAVING THE CHILDREN and the pigeons, Amedeo Modigliani continues putting one foot in front of another on his austere, morbid walk. Sad as the frozen branches of a birch tree, at the end of the street he catches sight of a large, restless, blazing fire. He notices that the drunken Cocteau is burning some strange kind of writings on it.

He stops.

VENI CREATOR SPIRITUS, Cocteau sings softly, placing some kind of strange, grotesque, wooden mask on his face, pale as quick-lime.

VENI CREATOR SPIRITUS, says the drunken Cocteau, dancing round the fire a ritual, fancy-dress, arrhythmic negro dance.

VENI CREATOR SPIRITUS, yells the drunken Cocteau, falling onto his knees, panting like a steam engine, broken, haggard, discarded like orange peel.

Four days before his death Amedeo Modigliani sees the burned paper forming a fine, pale, almost white powder of ash. He sees the smoke becoming a dove with a ring on its right leg bearing Gog and Magog, monsters that will appear on Judgment Day.

MY GOD, thinks Modigliani, this man is burning Dante. And, breathless, panting (we should not forget that he has been breathing through gills like a fish for two weeks now), he approaches the crushed Cocteau and places his hand on his shoulder.

HELLO, BIRD, says Cocteau, without raising his head.

Cocteau, Explanation

IN THE ROTONDE, Cocteau, relatively sober by now, explains to Amedeo that he burned Dante for the benefit of literature. Mon ami, he says, after Dante all our efforts in the field of literature become pointlessly comic and stupid.

And anything that makes human efforts pointless, comic or stupid deserves to be burned, doesn't it?

Amedeo, Soutine

PEOPLE ARE EITHER far away or they are not there at all, says Chaim Soutine that same afternoon to Amedeo, visibly moved as he supports the weight and the large, noble head of the Jew, the vagabond, the painter and sculptor Amedeo Modigliani.

Moved, he adjusts his deep, healthy breathing of a mature man to the feeble, grinding rasp of the sick man, still almost a boy.

On the pavement we see just one shadow.

The bigger, longer one.

On the pavement, as the two of them stagger, we observe, already predestined for destruction, the first shy, premature mark of the spring that will not come.

They are half-dead, trodden primroses, yellow and foolish as girlish modesty. On the pavement we notice wine vinegar, and the vomited sperm of dark-skinned Arab boys, we notice sharp stones, and the knives of lusty soldiers.

On the pavement we notice also a Pierrot with a hurdy-gurdy, an angel with a sword, and other such creatures as sleep by day and live by night.

On the pavement we notice the pavement.

People are either far away or they are not there at all, says Chaim Soutine, swearing forcefully, manfully, towards the town gates.

Amedeo, Port

A<small>T HALF PAST TWO</small> in the morning, not by chance, because that is the time when a poet dies every day, two friends see, astonished, A GREAT PORT.

They see LARGE, WHITE SHIPS.

Anchored and sluggish.

CARA ITALIA, Amedeo Modigliani is the first to react, running, his arms wide in the shape of a fan, like a crane's wings.

Chaim Soutine stands, in amazement, looking at the miracle.

CARA ITALIA, Amedeo Modigliani trembles and kneels, like some Flying Dutchman, without dry land, homeland or grave.

The boats are sluggish, asleep and silent.

Just like Divine mercy.

Evening, Hunger

O N THE TWENTY-FIRST OF JANUARY 1920 AD, wearing his Maltese Cross round his neck, Amedeo Modigliani, completely mad and hungry, hugs and kisses his wife Jeanne Hébuterne, sewing up her mouth, vagina and eyes with the silken threads of his enriched, consumptive saliva.

Many years later, Leopold Zborowski would talk about his drinking bouts lasting several days, and about one of Jeanne's festive dinners, when Amedeo Modigliani, quite overcome with joy and wine, picked up a hunting rifle and shot a wandering angel off the roof of a church. It was subsequently found to be nothing other than sea foam and feathers.

Grasshoppers from Algiers, the muzzles of smiling lions, a wash board, woodlice, tarot cards, the left ear of a Chinese mandarin, frozen boxes, a neon Madonna, tart grapes, drunken vanilla, barley shoots, an Austrian eagle, camels' blisters, space dust, little boys' testicles, tasteless bananas, artists' paints, dead fish from the Seine, big-eyed crabs, well-endowed monkeys and, of course, the salted tail of a young pheasant.

The menu, in other words, was as festive as it was strange.

The mood of the guests listed below was on a very enviable level:

Chaim Soutine, Leopold and Hanka Zborowski, Nekrasov, Baronness Béatrice, the Archangel Gabriel, Donna Clara the landlady, Sebastian—the one year-old son of the unfortunate Madame Carmelita, Max Jacob, Cocteau, Lolotte and Jeanne Hébuterne, tipsy brunette and hostess.

The thirteenth, at the head of the table, was Amedeo Modigliani, who in the first hours of morning, on the second day, quite overcome with joy and wine, fired a hunting rifle.

Any similarity with DA VINCI'S *LAST SUPPER* is unintentional and fortuitous, announced Leopold Zborowski finally.

Towns, Tears

I SEE A MILLION light-bearing towns, said Amedeo
Modigliani tipsily, accompanying his guests to the
door, I see Rome, the Pope's capital, I see Madrid, city
of bulls and poets, I see drunken Moscow, I see large
ships spreading their sails in Barcelona, I see the shots
fired by Gavrilo Princip in Sarajevo in 1914, I see
the burning eyes of virgins in Naples, I see syphilitics
waltzing in Vienna, I see a flaming field of poppies in
my native Livorno, I see a bare, ugly hill in Jerusalem,
I see crazy hatters in London, I see a fly and a spider
dancing a tango in Buenos Aires, I see death as a regu-
lar phenomenon in Santiago, I see avenues of mighty
bearded trees in Budapest, I see aggressive negro
music in the docks of New York, I see Whitman's lilac
in Washington, I see women swimming in Avignon,
I see a young moon with its belly turned towards
sleeping Granada, I see fat German rabble drunkenly
whooping in the streets of Munich, I see saints, cows
and firecrackers in Bombay, I see a crowd of mina-
rets against the sky above Istanbul, I see the sleeping

roofs of Prague by night, I see the sweaty rifles of the Bolsheviks on the white face of Saint Petersburg, I see the walls of the Bastille, I see a mustachioed sergeant in Berlin yelling 'SIEG HEIL', his throat slit, I see all the President's men in the centre of Havana, I see twenty-three drunken carpet-makers in front of the gates of Katmandu, I see juicy women's breasts in Hamburg windows, I see the great babbling tongues of plump café owners from Lyon, I see the bird of the south in Palermo, I see lovers from Verona, I see a heap of rat-like faces in the sewage system of Copenhagen, I see unreasonable delight on the faces of peasants on Saint Valentine's Day in Caracas, I see Chicago, and I see:

I SEE THAT THE ENTIRE WORLD IS PARIS.

AND I AM ABOUT TO LEAVE IT.

GOODNIGHT TO YOU, CAMARADES.

A VERY GOODNIGHT.

The people leave, turning up their collars, blowing on their fingers, coughing, in the almost grave-like silence. GOODNIGHT BIRD, says Cocteau, who is the last to leave, carrying a litre of wine and some un-finished poems in his pocket. And, leaning on the doorpost, Amedeo Modigliani, the cursed painter from Livorno, stands, shivering with cold, but says nothing.

He is silent.

And his silence seems to explain everything.

Amedeo, Death

WHO KILLED THE CRANES, mutters Amedeo Modigliani who has just woken up. He shivers as he inserts his narrow, pointed little Jewish backside into his frayed trousers, unstitched in places, the pockets filled with unpainted faces, unspent coins and as yet un-sniffed cocaine.

Cranes, says Jeanne, what cranes. Last night I dreamed only of trumpets.

These two dead cranes, says the painter going up to her, on the threshold of our apartment, says the painter, caressing the front of Jeanne's hair, because hair too has a front and a back but it does not remotely matter.

THE OMENS CANNOT BE GOOD.

So saying, he puts his easel and paintbox under his arm and goes outside.

Perhaps I'll even paint something he mutters into his beard.

However, he does not get further than the first bistro.

Both God and the Devil play the same key.

And that key is B-Minor, says Amedeo Modigliani, inhaling the gaze of a woman sitting at the bar.

She is pale, almost white, like a lily.

She is called Ludmilla.

She is blonde, slender, tall, thin as a northerner.

FUCK YOUR EASEL, she says.

Because, when he caught sight of that heady, white beauty, he was blinded, and he raised both his left and his right hand to his eyes in a sudden spasm, leaving his armpit open. So the easel fell and rebounded from the bistro floor dully, dead, like rotten fruit.

FUCK YOUR EASEL, she says.

Looking him straight in the eye.

And Amedeo Modigliani is looking at her feet, wild, barely captured in her exceptional shoes, he is looking at her long, waxy calves, her knees and ever upwards.

He sees her narrow hips, too narrow; her little breasts like two drops of honey, her snake-like neck and hair—MON DIEU—blonde.

I am Amedeo, the painter barely manages to utter, knocking back a cold vodka, a bit insipid, watery, as he swims in the sharp gaze of Ludmilla's large eyes which look as though all the blue of the heavens has poured into them.

I was on my way home and just happened to turn towards Montparnasse. It's very sad here, says Ludmilla sipping a tepid beer, in tiny, staccato gulps like a nightingale, leaving, naughtily, a garland of foam on her upper lip, so that she looks like a rough, drunken woodcutter.

Forgive me, that means you are not from round here, says Amedeo Modigliani stuck like a polyp to his glass and the bar.

No, Ludmilla shakes her head, I come from the sky.

And her words slide, rebounding from the flat surface of the bar, only to evaporate, together with the nicotine smoke somewhere towards the ceiling or somewhat higher. Forever.

Because everything that happens need not necessarily be forgotten.

SOMETHING, SOMETHING SMALL, REMAINS TO BE REMEMBERED.

And tomorrow, she smiles, I'm taking you to the cranes.

She resembles the pitiless face of death, which everyone carries on their right shoulder.

She looks like a dream in colour, like large bunches of our forebears, who did not die in vain.

Ludmilla looks like all those things that happen once in a lifetime or never. Particularly if you are a Jew and you are drunk.

And finally:

See you again, says Ludmilla in English as she goes, it is English with the heavy accent of a chronic foreigner, leaving behind a festive, cobwebby smell of rotting apples.

See you soon.

In the sky, says Ludmilla, leaving.

Her spine a little bent.

She is pale, almost white, like a lily.

She is blonde, slender, tall, thin as a northerner.

He is left alone.

There are still a few long winter hours until midnight.

Quite enough for another round of drinks.

Perhaps a bit more.

Amedeo Modigliani (1884-1920) decides to get drunk.

He saw how a light flickered on and the two halves of a window opened out, somebody, made weak and thin by the height and the distance, leant suddenly far out from it and stretched his arms out even further. Who was that? A friend? A good person? Somebody who was taking part? Somebody who wanted to help? Was he alone? Was it everyone? Would anyone help? Were there objections that had been forgotten? There must have been some. The logic cannot be refuted, but someone who wants to live will not resist it. Where was the judge he'd never seen? Where was the high court he had never reached? He raised both hands and spread out all his fingers.

But the hands of one of the gentleman were laid on K's throat, while the other pushed the knife deep into his heart and twisted it there, twice. As his eyesight failed, K saw the two gentlemen cheek by cheek, close in front of his face, watching the result.

'Like a dog!' he said, it was as if the shame of it should outlive him.

FRANZ KAFKA *The Trial*

Post Scriptum

A MEDEO MODIGLIANI DIED in the night between the twenty-fourth and twenty-fifth of January in the paupers' Hôpital de la Charité. The day after his death, his wife, Jeanne Hébuterne, in the eighth month of pregnancy, threw herself out of a window at her parents' house.

According to the medical report, Modigliani died by choking on his own blood.

The last thing he said before he closed his exhausted noble eyes, was:

ITALIA, CARA ITALIA.

Acknowledgments

The Outsider by Albert Camus, translated by Stuart Gilbert (Hamish Hamilton 1946) translation copyright 1946 by Stuart Gilbert. Reproduced by permission of Penguin Books Ltd.

The Stranger by Albert Camus, translated by Stuart Gilbert, copyright 1946 and renewed 1974 by Alfred A Knopf, a division of Random House, Inc. Used by permission of Alfred A Knopf, a division of Random House, Inc.

Selected Poems by Jorge Luis Borges edited by Alexander Coleman (Allen Lane The Penguin Press 1999). Copyright © Maria Kodoma 1999. Translation copyright © Alan S Trueblood 1999. Reproduced by permission of Penguin Books Ltd.

Selected Poems by Jorge Luis Borges, edited by Alexander Coleman. Used by permission of Viking Penguin, a division of Penguin Group USA. Copyright © 1999

PUSHKIN PRESS

Pushkin Press was founded in 1997, and publishes novels, essays, memoirs, children's books—everything from timeless classics to the urgent and contemporary.

Our books represent exciting, high-quality writing from around the world: we publish some of the twentieth century's most widely acclaimed, brilliant authors such as Stefan Zweig, Marcel Aymé, Teffi, Antal Szerb, Gaito Gazdanov and Yasushi Inoue, as well as compelling and award-winning contemporary writers, including Andrés Neuman, Edith Pearlman, Eka Kurniawan, Ayelet Gundar-Goshen and Chigozie Obioma.

Pushkin Press publishes the world's best stories, to be read and read again. To discover more, visit www.pushkinpress.com.

═══

THE SPECTRE OF ALEXANDER WOLF
GAITO GAZDANOV

'A mesmerising work of literature' Antony Beevor

SUMMER BEFORE THE DARK
VOLKER WEIDERMANN

'For such a slim book to convey with such poignancy the extinction of a generation of "Great Europeans" is a triumph' *Sunday Telegraph*

MESSAGES FROM A LOST WORLD
STEFAN ZWEIG

'At a time of monetary crisis and political disorder... Zweig's celebration of the brotherhood of peoples reminds us that there is another way' *The Nation*

THE EVENINGS
GERARD REVE

'Not only a masterpiece but a cornerstone manqué of modern European literature' Tim Parks, *Guardian*

BINOCULAR VISION
EDITH PEARLMAN
'A genius of the short story' Mark Lawson, *Guardian*

IN THE BEGINNING WAS THE SEA
TOMÁS GONZÁLEZ
'Smoothly intriguing narrative, with its touches of sinister,
Patricia Highsmith-like menace' *Irish Times*

BEWARE OF PITY
STEFAN ZWEIG
'Zweig's fictional masterpiece' *Guardian*

THE ENCOUNTER
PETRU POPESCU
'A book that suggests new ways of looking at the world
and our place within it' *Sunday Telegraph*

WAKE UP, SIR!
JONATHAN AMES
'The novel is extremely funny but it is also sad and
poignant, and almost incredibly clever' *Guardian*

THE WORLD OF YESTERDAY
STEFAN ZWEIG
'*The World of Yesterday* is one of the greatest memoirs of the twentieth
century, as perfect in its evocation of the world Zweig loved, as it is
in its portrayal of how that world was destroyed' David Hare

WAKING LIONS
AYELET GUNDAR-GOSHEN
'A literary thriller that is used as a vehicle to explore big
moral issues. I loved everything about it' *Daily Mail*

FOR A LITTLE WHILE
RICK BASS
'Bass is, hands down, a master of the short form, creating in a few pages
a natural world of mythic proportions' *New York Times Book Review*